Haffertee Hamster's New House

Haffertee is a soft-toy hamster. Ma Diamond made him for her little girl, Yolanda (Diamond Yo), when her real pet hamster died.

In this book – the second in the series – Haffertee meets old friends and makes some new ones as he explores Hillside House. In the process, he learns a good deal about himself, and grows up enough to be given a place of his own.

The charm of the stories lies in the funny, lovable character of Haffertee himself, and in the special place God has in the affections of Diamond Yo and her family.

The
Diamond
Family

Fran   Ma

Diamond Yo
with
Haffertee and
Howl Out

Pops

Mark

Chris.

Haffertee Hamster's New House

By Janet and John Perkins
Illustrations by Gillian Gaze

A LION PAPERBACK

Copyright © 1977 Janet and John Perkins

Published by
Lion Publishing
Icknield Way, Tring, Herts, England
ISBN 0 85648 491 1
Albatross Books
PO Box 320, Sutherland, NSW 2232, Australia
ISBN 0 86760 373 9

First edition 1977
Second edition 1979
This edition 1982

Cover picture and illustrations by Gillian Gaze
Copyright © 1977 Lion Publishing

Printed and bound in Great Britain by
Collins, Glasgow

Contents

It all began when Yo's pet hamster died.
To cheer her up, Ma Diamond made a ginger-
and-white soft-toy hamster. The new
Haffertee Hamster Diamond proved to be
quite a character – inquisitive, funny
and lovable. From his home in Yo's
bedroom – shared with his friend Howl Owl
and a strange collection of toys – he set
out to explore Hillside House and meet the
family: Ma and Pops Diamond and Yo's older
brothers and sister, Chris, Fran and Mark.
His adventures in the house and garden, and
the World Outside are told in four books of
stories: *Haffertee Hamster Diamond, Haffertee
Hamster's New House, Haffertee Goes Exploring* and
Haffertee's First Christmas.

Haffertee is Not Himself

It was a lovely morning. Haffertee and Howl Owl were sitting quietly on the top of Yo's new desk, talking about the sunshine and listening to some birds chattering away on the fence at the end of the garden.

Suddenly there was a rush of fur and a flash of white whisker. The three Purrswell kittens, Dominic, Tina and Smudge had arrived on the desk top. They were all playing happily together and pretending to fight.

Haffertee and Howl watched for a while and then went on enjoying the sunshine.

The birds had all gone! The kittens were jumping about all over the place.

9

'Hello, Haffertee,' said Smudge politely. 'Can you jump?'

Haffertee considered the question carefully and then said, 'Not very well, but I can always try.'

Smudge stood back from the edge of the desk. 'Watch this,' she said proudly, and she sprang away out into nothing and landed with a plop! on Diamond Yo's bed.

Haffertee watched carefully. He was very impressed. 'Goodness me!' he said. 'That was a great jump.'

'Watch this, then,' said Tina as she launched herself into the air. Right across to the bed she flew and landed with another plop! next to Smudge.

'And this,' said a third flying kitten, as Dominic leapt to join the other two. All three of them started bouncing and jumping on Yo's bed.

Dominic turned right round and called back to Haffertee. 'Come on, now, Haffertee. Show us how you can jump.'

Haffertee wasn't at all sure that he could jump that far. It seemed such a long way. He walked to the edge of the desk and peered over. It looked a very long way down.

'Don't tell us you are afraid,' called Smudge.
'You can't jump at all,' said Tina.

'Hamsters aren't much good at anything,' teased Dominic.

Haffertee didn't like that. 'I'll show them,' he grunted fiercely to himself. 'I'll show them!'

He walked back from the edge of the desk, took a deep breath and then began to run towards the gap between the desk and the bed. When he reached the edge of the desk he flung himself out into the emptiness and closed his eyes.

Howl Owl kept *his* eyes open. What he saw made him shudder. Haffertee got about halfway across the open space and then began to fall head-over-heels-over-head-over-heels. Down and down and . . . thump!

Silence. Not even a squeak.

Howl hurried to the edge and looked down. Haffertee was a sad little heap of ginger-and-white on the floor below. He wasn't moving. Howl quickly fluttered down.

The three kittens jumped off the bed for a closer look. But Haffertee just lay still.

Howl was just about to go for help, when help arrived.

Diamond Yo came into the room. She took one look at Haffertee and ran across to him. She picked him up gently and started smoothing his fur.

'Haffertee, Haffertee,' she said anxiously. 'Are you all right?'

At first there was no sound or stir. Then, after a second or two of stroking and smoothing and tending, Haffertee opened his eyes and groaned a little. Rather carefully, he began to move about in Yo's hand. At last, as nothing seemed to be broken, he managed to stand up straight and look around.

'Where am I?' he asked, rather weakly. 'What hit me?'

Howl started to explain. He was very glad to see that Haffertee was not badly hurt.

'Don't you remember?' he said. 'The Purrswell kittens were teasing you, and you tried to jump from the desk to the bed.'

'You did *what*?' asked Yo, not really believing what Howl had just said. 'You did what?'

'I tried to jump from the desk to the bed,' said Haffertee, hanging his head. 'I was halfway across when I stopped.'

'Stopped and fell down, you mean,' said Yo with a smile. 'You aren't a kitten, you know. There are some things you were made to do and some things you weren't. God made each of us in a special way to do different things. You've never heard of a lion who sang like a bird, have you? Or a pig who could fly?'

'No,' said Haffertee – the idea made him giggle.

'Well, hamsters aren't made to jump like kittens. You have to be yourself, Haffertee. You can't really be anybody else, no matter how hard you try.'

With that, Yo put Haffertee gently back on top of her desk. Howl Owl fluttered up to join him. He looked his little friend carefully up and down.

'You would look funny with a kitten's tail,' he said at last. 'Very funny indeed!'

The Magic Sticks

Diamond Yo had a box of magic sticks. At least, that is what she had just told Haffertee.

'Look,' she said. 'Look very carefully.'

Yo opened the little box which she had in her hand and took out a small wooden stick. It wasn't quite as long as her little finger and it had a black top.

'There,' said Yo with great pride. 'That is a match.'

'A match,' said Haffertee. 'A match. What do you want that for?'

'Aha!' said Yo, mysteriously. 'I'm going to show you something.'

Haffertee waited and watched. Yo began to scratch the black top of the match against the strong side of the box. It made a very funny noise. It spluttered and crackled and sizzled and then the black head disappeared.

'There. Look at that!' said Yo, in great excitement.

Haffertee looked. He couldn't see anything at all! Then, suddenly, there was a long grey string of smoke curling up to the ceiling.

'That was a flame,' said Yo. 'It came out of that black top.'

'But I didn't see anything at all,' said Haffertee, in surprise. 'Just a long grey string of smoke.'

Diamond Yo looked at him carefully. Then she took another stick out of the box and rubbed it against the box-side. There was a spluttering and sizzling and crackling again. But still Haffertee couldn't see anything at all. Nothing, that is, except the long grey string of smoke that came later.

'See it?' called Yo, in her excitement. 'Did you see that lovely flame?'

Haffertee was beginning to feel disappointed. 'No, I didn't see anything at all,' he said again.

Yo came over to Haffertee and looked back at the place where she had been standing. Haffertee just wasn't paying attention, she was sure. Then she understood what was the matter. Haffertee had been looking

15

towards the window, and the flame had not shown up against the bright sunshine streaming into the room. No wonder he had not seen anything. Yo had an idea.

'Come over here,' she said. 'Let's get under the bed.'

'Under the bed?' squeaked Haffertee. 'Under the bed! Whatever do we want to get under the bed for?'

'Well,' said Yo, explaining. 'It is much darker under there and you will be able to see the lovely colours of the flame I make with these matches!'

Haffertee wasn't too sure about Yo's magic sticks. They didn't seem quite safe. And he didn't much like the idea of getting too close. But he wanted to see the flame, so he crawled in under the bed and sat down close to Yo. There wasn't room for Yo to sit up – she had to lie flat on her tummy. She held the box in front of her, and a match in her hand, ready to strike the top against the box-side.

'Now then,' she said, firmly. 'Just you watch.' And she started the spluttering, crackling and sizzling all over again.

This time Haffertee did see the flame. His nervousness vanished. He leant forward. The flame was very hot, but even this did not bother him. It was so very pretty. It started yellow and then changed to red and blue and then back to yellow again. It burnt its way down the stick a little, then disappeared into nowhere. Haffertee sighed as the long grey string of smoke curled up into the mattress.

'There,' said Yo. 'Wasn't that fun?' Haffertee nodded. It certainly was.

Yo took another match and started another flame. This time it was even bigger and longer than the first one. The colours were bright and beautiful and the stick burned on and on. This time the grey smoke was all around Haffertee, making him blink and cough. And before he could see what was happening, the flame had jumped on to the bedcover!

In no time at all, it seemed, flames and colours were jumping in and out and over and over and round and round. The whole bed seemed to be one flame. Haffertee scuttled out from under the bed coughing and spluttering.

Yo wriggled backwards in panic. She grabbed Haffertee and ran to the top of the stairs.

'Mummy! Mummy!' she screamed. 'Come quickly. My bed is on fire!'

'Howl! Howl! Wake up,' shouted Haffertee. 'The house is a flame!'

Ma Diamond raced upstairs. Pops Diamond took

the steps two at a time. And all the while Howl Owl hooted and tooted.

Ma and Pops took one look at Yo, then rushed past her into the bedroom. It was no time for questions. While Ma closed the window, Pops ran to the bathroom and soaked the towels under the tap. Then he rushed back into Yo's room and they both began beating at the flames with the wet towels.

There was a hissing and a spitting and a bubbling – and slowly the flames died down and the steam floated out.

Yo and Haffertee sat still outside the room looking very shaken and sorry for themselves. When Ma and Pops came out at last, they both looked tired and a bit sad.

'Yo,' said Pops. 'Didn't we warn you not to play with matches?'

'Yes,' said Yo, so softly you could hardly hear her. 'You did.'

'Didn't we tell you how dangerous they are?' said Ma.

Yo nodded her head and began to cry. 'I'm sorry, Mummy,' she said, through the tears. 'I didn't listen to what you said and now look what I've done.'

They all looked back into the room at the black sheets and the wet carpet and the marked wall. Haffertee felt like crying, too.

Pops knelt down beside Yo and took hold of her hand.

'I'm sorry, Daddy,' she said, gripping his hand. 'I truly am.'

'You really *must* do what we say!' said Pops. 'Why, you could have set the whole house on fire . . . '

'If Yo does what Ma and Pops say, and I do what Yo says, then Ma and Pops . . . ' Haffertee was trying hard to be helpful, but he couldn't quite work this one out.

'Children should obey their parents, God says so,' Yo said firmly.

'That's right,' said Pops gently. 'And God forgives us when we're truly sorry. So now it's all over Yo.'

'What's all over Yo?' asked Haffertee.

Yo smiled a wobbly smile. Funny old Haff. She blew her nose hard, and went to get some soapy water from the kitchen. She felt better already.

Frank the Tank

The Dreadful Fire was almost – but not quite – forgotten. Yo had worked hard helping Ma Diamond wash and clean her room, and Haffertee had helped, too. Everything was back to normal again.

Howl Owl was over by the desk in the corner of Yo's room, counting slowly. '1 . . . 2 . . . 3 . . . 4 . . .' They were playing Hide-and-Seek.

Haffertee knew just where he was going to hide – in the cupboard by the wall. He had already hidden

in Yo's clothes cupboard and in the Toy Cupboard. But he hadn't been in that cupboard near the wall before.

Howl Owl was still counting quietly. '14 … 15 … 16 … 17 … '

Haffertee pulled the door open and went inside. He closed the door behind him just in time. Howl had finished counting and was out looking.

It was very warm in the cupboard and at first it was very dark, too. After a minute or two Haffertee's eyes got used to the darkness.

There right in front of him was a big barrel! A big round barrel … with arms and legs like pipes coming and going in all directions. The barrel was surrounded by piles and piles of clean clothes.

Haffertee stood quite still and looked. He had to bend over backwards to look up as far as the top of the barrel, it was so tall. He could just make out a round smiling face with a very large colourful bow tie underneath.

'Gosh!' said Haffertee, without thinking. 'You are fat.'

The barrel didn't move but you could feel that it was hurt. 'Do you always stare like that?' said a soft, bubbly voice. 'Are you always so rude?'

Haffertee didn't know what to say. He had never heard a barrel speak before.

'This is my home,' went on the bubbly voice, 'and you didn't even bother to knock before you came in. Where are your manners? It is good that I am not a fierce tank.'

'I'm very sorry,' squeaked Haffertee, quite taken

aback. 'I didn't know anyone lived in here.'

'Who are you?' said the bubbly voice, rather sternly. 'And why have you come in here?'

Haffertee hurried to explain. 'I am Haffertee Hamster,' he said. 'I live with Yo and the Diamond family – and I am hiding in here from my friend Howl Owl. We are playing Hide-and-Seek.'

The barrel was silent for a moment or two. When he spoke again he seemed much more friendly.

'Any friend of Howl Owl's is a friend of mine,' he bubbled kindly. 'I am Frank the Tank and you are welcome to my cupboard now and any time. I am

full of nice hot water, and I air all the clothes Ma Diamond brings to me. It's my job to make the water hot. Hot baths for all the family. Hot water for Ma to do the washing. And warm, clean clothes for everyone, to keep them happy. It's a very important job. Just you come in here and sit down if ever you feel cold and wet. I shall be very pleased to warm and dry you.'

Haffertee was feeling lovely and warm and soft and dry already. He had almost forgotten the game of Hide-and-Seek when Frank began to sing in his watery, bubbly voice.

'I make the water lovely and warm.
I share my room with the clothes.
The ironing comes in on a Tuesday
And I keep it aired till it goes.'

Frank stopped singing, and a slow, happy smile spread all over his face. He liked making people happy. Everyone likes hot baths and clean, warm clothes.

Haffertee secretly thought it was all a bit dull. How could anyone bear to stay still in the same place all the time, just being hot? Then he remembered what Yo had said. Hamsters weren't made to be kittens – or Tanks! Frank was just being himself. Haffertee was pleased he'd thought of that. Then he remembered the game.

He smiled politely at Frank. 'Thank you,' he said. 'I think I must go now. Howl Owl will be wondering where I have got to. I will certainly come and see you again soon. Good Day to you, Frank.'

Frank rumbled his 'Goodbye' and went on bubbling away to himself.

Haffertee stepped out of the cupboard and closed the door. 'A talking tank,' he murmured. 'Whatever next?'

'Got you,' said a deep voice right behind his ear. 'Got you. Now it is my turn to hide.'

Howl Owl fluttered away across the room and Haffertee went over to the desk in the corner, and began to count slowly up to 20 . . .

A Place of His Own

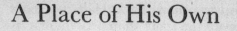

Diamond Yo had just come bouncing in from school. She ran up to her room, and opened the door.

'Hello, Haffertee,' she called, as she tossed her school bag on to the bed. 'Have you had a nice day?'

'No,' said Haffertee, very sharply. 'I have not!'

Yo looked at Haffertee with a puzzled frown on her face. She hadn't heard him speak like that before. She thought she would try again. 'Have you had a . . .'

'No, I haven't,' burst out Haffertee. 'Now will you please go away and leave me alone!'

Yo was very surprised. She shrugged her shoulders and went downstairs to the kitchen. She wanted to find out more, but she felt that Haffertee was best left alone for a bit as he had asked – at least until tea-time.

Haffertee had the room to himself again. He sat on the bed and held his head in his hands. He was feeling cross and out of sorts. It had been coming on for days. He thought he knew what was wrong.

'It's that silly old pillowcase,' he muttered. 'Why can't I have a place of my own like everyone else? Frank the Tank has a whole cupboard to himself. Howl Owl has his own shelf. I want a proper place of my own.'

Diamond Yo was coming back. Haffertee could hear her coming up the stairs thumpety-thumpety-thumpety-thump.

'Tea-time, Haffertee,' she called, as she came into the room. 'Come down and have some tea with us. Perhaps you'll feel better after that.'

'Don't want any tea,' said Haffertee gruffly, through his paws. 'Don't feel like any tea.'

'Oh! Haffertee,' said Yo gently. 'Whatever is the matter with you? You don't normally talk to me like that. What is making you so upset?'

Haffertee turned away.

'Oh, come on,' said Yo, firmly. 'We're friends, aren't we? We can tell each other things.'

Haffertee turned back ever so ever so slowly, and then he nodded. 'I suppose so,' he said rather grudgingly.

'Then tell me what is the matter,' said Yo.

Haffertee took a deep breath: 'I don't want to sleep in that silly old pillowcase any more,' he blurted out. 'Everybody else in the house has a place of their

26

own. You and Chris have rooms of your own. Frank the Tank has a cupboard of his own and Howl Owl has a shelf of his own. That's what I want. A place of my own.' Yo lifted him up gently in her hands. She looked at him carefully and then put him down again on the bed. She felt a little bit hurt.

Haffertee belonged in the pillowcase. 'He has always slept in the pillowcase,' she thought. 'It is the right place for Haffertee.' And yet . . . perhaps he should have a place of his own now. She nodded her head as she thought about that a little more.

'Hmmmmm!' she said at last. 'Hmmmmmmm! Ahhhhh! Yes!'

At last it seemed that she had made up her mind. 'Right,' she said. 'Right. Is that what you really want, Haffertee?'

'Yes,' said Haffertee quickly. 'I do.'

'Then,' said Yo, 'that is what you shall have. After tea we'll find a nice cardboard box and we'll cut out a door and some windows and we'll find something soft for you to sleep on and we'll fix you up with a table and some chairs and . . . ' She paused to take breath, ' . . . and in no time at all you can have a place of your very own. We'll call it Haffertee Hamster's Own Box.'

Haffertee was delighted. He smiled at Yo and went down to tea.

He was even more delighted after tea.

Yo found an old cardboard box up in the loft and brought it down to her room. She began to cut out windows and a door.

Howl Owl fetched some chairs and a table from

the Toy Cupboard, and a nice warm soft duster from the pile behind Frank the Tank. Together they arranged the table and the chairs and smoothed the soft duster into one corner for a bed.

Haffertee just watched. Then, when everything was ready, he moved into his Very Own Box. He liked it very much. He settled himself into a comfortable chair and began to sing . . .

'It's nice to have a cardboard box
To call my very own.
To leave my friends and all outside
And sit here in my brand-new home.
Who's afraid in a cardboard box?
The place I come to rest.
My own bed and my own armchair.
That's what I love best.'

'Ahhhh!' yawned Haffertee, as he finished his song. 'Ahhh! It's time for bed . . . ' and he lay down happily on the warm soft duster in the corner. 'Goodnight, everyone.'

Yo and Howl Owl moved quietly away. Howl fluttered up on to his shelf and Yo climbed into bed. Haffertee seemed very pleased with his new home.

But somehow he just couldn't sleep.

He felt lonely all on his own.

He tossed and turned and twisted and thought. It was no good. He just couldn't sleep.

Yo was almost asleep herself when she felt something soft brush past her face. 'Haffertee,' she whispered. 'Is that you, Haffertee?'

'Yes,' said Haffertee softly. 'It's me.'

'Don't you like your new bed?' she asked. 'It looked very comfortable to me.'

'Er . . . Well . . . Yes . . . ' stammered Haffertee. 'Yes. I do like my own bed but, er . . . you see . . . it's a bit lonely in that box and, er . . . if you don't mind I'd like to sleep in your pillowcase.'

Yo smiled to herself. 'Of course,' she said happily and snuggled Haffertee into his old place inside the pillowcase.

'Thank you,' said Haffertee. 'Thank you very much.' And he was asleep before Yo could say any more. She was very glad to have Haffertee back with her. She had felt rather lonely, too.

'Thank you for Haffertee, God,' she said with a sleepy yawn, finishing her goodnight prayer. 'Thank you very much!'

The Mirror on the Desk

Haffertee Hamster Diamond was standing in front of the mirror. Howl Owl had gone off for the day to see some of his relations, and Diamond Yo was at school.

Haffertee was taking a very long look at himself. His ginger fur was beautifully brushed and shining. The white fur was spotless and fluffy.

His ears were standing up straight and firm and his whiskers were stretching and twitching.

'V-e-r-y handsome,' Haffertee thought. He was rather full of himself today. Full of food, too, from his recent visit to the kitchen. He yawned. The room was very quiet. Perhaps he would just sit down for a bit . . .

Before he knew it, he was fast asleep and dreaming. He was standing in front of the mirror, admiring himself.

'Good morning,' he said to the figure in the mirror. 'What a fine fellow you are!'

He didn't expect an answer. But he got one. The figure in the mirror smiled, and then said, 'Good morning, Haffertee.'

Haffertee gasped.

The figure in the mirror moved a little to one side. 'I am Ginger Nutt,' he said, politely, 'and I have something to show you.'

Haffertee was slowly recovering from the shock of hearing the mirror speak. 'Oh!' he managed to squeak. 'Have you?'

'Come and see,' said the figure, beckoning to Haffertee. Haffertee moved closer.

'Come on,' said Ginger Nutt. 'Step inside.'

Haffertee stepped carefully inside the mirror and found himself in a large room which seemed to be full of shoeboxes. Shoeboxes in lines with a little white label at the end of each box.

'Over here,' called Ginger Nutt. 'Take a look at this.' Haffertee stepped over to the shoebox where Ginger Nutt was standing. Inside the box, lying on a piece of soft carpet, was a ginger-and-white soft-toy hamster. He was fast asleep.

'What's he doing in there?' asked Haffertee in a whisper.

'Look at the label,' answered Ginger Nutt.

Haffertee looked at the label and read:

Sandy Jim: found in a ditch in Clapton Lane

'We found him in a ditch last winter,' said Ginger

Nutt. 'He was all wet and muddy and covered in oil. He had no home to go to, so we have been looking after him ever since. His fur is still bluey-green because of the oil.'

Haffertee thought about that for a moment and then moved along to the next box. The label said:

Ears torn by brambles: found in Walton Woods

'He has been here some time now,' said Ginger Nutt.

Haffertee looked carefully at the torn ears. Then he moved along the line of boxes, looking into each one and reading the labels. Ginger Nutt explained what had happened to the little ginger-and-white soft-toy hamster in each box. All of them had had some sad adventure.

Some had very dirty fur.

Some had very little fur at all.

Some had torn ears and paws.

Some had lost part of their stuffing.

One of them had lost both eyes and nearly all his fur. Haffertee looked at them sadly. He was feeling rather funny inside.

He began to think. He had nice clean fur and his ears were straight and firm. He had two good eyes to see with . . . and a good home and some very nice friends and . . .

Ginger Nutt broke in. 'These little hamsters are all so much less than themselves,' he said. 'You should be glad you have Yo to love you, and a good home and lots of friends . . . '

'Hello!' said a very familiar voice, right in Haffertee's ear. 'Have you been sleeping *all* day?'

It was Diamond Yo, home from school.

Haffertee came to with a start and rubbed his eyes. He looked around. Ginger Nutt was nowhere to be seen. There was no sign of the row of shoeboxes. And when he looked in the mirror, all he could see was a picture of himself!

Haffertee told Yo all about his dream. 'Ginger Nutt was right,' he finished. 'I *am* a very happy hamster. I'm glad I'm Haffertee Hamster Diamond, with you to love me, and Howl Owl and everyone.'

Yo poggled his ears. 'Dear old Haffertee,' she said. 'I do love you. Now, how about some tea?'

Haffertee Just Can't Wait!

There was a strange whirring and shurring noise coming from Ma Diamond's room. Haffertee had heard it before but he had never taken much notice of it.

Today it sounded special.

Today he had nothing to do.

And even a strange whirring and shurring noise sounds special on a day when there is nothing to do.

Haffertee made his way across the upstairs landing to Ma Diamond's room and knocked on the door. There was no answer.

He waited until the noise had stopped and then knocked again.

'Come in,' said Ma, 'and mind your step.'

Haffertee did mind his step. He had to. There were pieces of white paper and blue material all over the place.

'Whatever are you doing?' he asked as he made his way carefully between the pieces.

'I'm trying to make a party dress for Yo,' said Ma. 'But I'm afraid it's taking me much longer than I thought.'

Haffertee was looking round the room carefully.

'Where does the whirring noise come from?' he asked.

Ma nodded her head towards a strange-looking black machine standing just near the edge of the table.

'That's my sewing-machine,' she said. 'It's a bit old now but it still works hard.'

She put her foot down on a switch on the floor and the whirring and shurring began again. Part of the black machine was going round and round, part of it was going up and down, and a reel of blue cotton was dancing on top.

'Does that make the dress?' asked Haffertee, watching the machine eat up some of the blue material.

'Yes,' said Ma, quickly. 'I just keep sewing the parts together and before long we have a nice new dress.'

Haffertee stood looking at the pieces and the machine and thinking about the nice new dress. 'I do like that soft blue material,' he said, after standing and watching for some time. 'Can I make myself a coat?'

Ma turned and looked at him carefully. He obviously meant it. She thought for a moment. Then she said, 'I'm afraid I can't stop to help you make a coat now, Haffertee, but if you will wait a minute or two I'll finish this dress and then we can make one together.'

But Haffertee wasn't really listening. He was thinking how very smart he would look in a nice new blue coat. He was much too excited to wait – even a minute or two. 'It's all right,' he said firmly. 'I can manage by myself.'

Ma Diamond shrugged her shoulders. 'You won't

be able to use the machine,' she said. 'That really is too hard for you, but if you do the sewing with this needle and cotton then you might be able to make a coat.'

She picked a needle out of her needle-case and threaded some cotton into it. 'Here you are,' she said. 'And here are some large white buttons. They will look very nice on a blue coat.'

Ma picked up some small pieces of the soft blue material and handed them to Haffertee. 'There,' she said. 'You can make your coat from these.'

'Thank you very much,' said Haffertee, in a hurry. And he trotted back to Diamond Yo's room with the pieces of material, the needle and cotton, the scissors and the big white buttons. He was very anxious to get on with the job.

The scissors were soon flashing away.

Snip. Snap. Snip. Snap. Snip. Snap.

He cut out the pieces for the front and the back and the sleeves. It didn't take long. He would have the coat made in no time at all! When he had finished the cutting he picked up the pieces and held them against himself to measure them. They didn't seem to be quite the right length, but that could be put right when the coat was finished. Just a little bit off here and there.

Haffertee picked up the needle and began to sew. He sewed this piece to that piece, and that piece to the other piece. It was much harder than he had thought.
. Now for the buttons.

A few more sews and, presto! The coat was finished. Haffertee was very pleased with himself. He just couldn't wait to try it on.

But, do you know, when he tried to put it on he just couldn't get into it. He struggled and twisted and tussled and turned. It was no good. The coat just did not fit. He had sewn the back to the front and the sleeves across each other. The buttons were in the wrong places and there were no buttonholes at all. The coat just wasn't a coat. It was more like a cushion-cover with buttons all over it. Haffertee was very sad and sorry for himself. The very first time he had tried to make something, and he had made a terrible mess of it.

Yo found him, still very sad and sorry for himself, later in the afternoon. She seemed to know just what had happened, and when she spoke she was very gentle.

'You should have waited a little while, Haffertee, and let Mummy help you. She would have done, you know. She just couldn't help you then. She was so busy. A coat is a difficult thing to make. You can't expect to do it without some help, especially the very first time. You can't do everything on your own, you know. No one can.'

Haffertee hung his head. Yo was right. He should
have waited and listened. He was sorry about that.
He picked up the blue bundle sewn all over with
large white buttons and looked at it thoughtfully.

'Perhaps we could use it as a blanket for the
Purrswell kittens,' he said, with a half-smile. 'At least
it won't be wasted then. I think I'll try and make a
handkerchief next time.'

'What a good idea,' said Ma, who had just come
into the room. 'But I have a few minutes to spare now,
Haffertee. We can undo your stitches and see if we
can't make you a proper new blue coat, if you like.'

39

Haffertee did like. He thought it was a wonderful idea. So that is what they did. The two of them spent a lot of time in Ma's room with the whirring and shurring sewing-machine. And when Haffertee came out he was wearing a new blue coat with lovely white buttons. He really did look smart!

The Body on the Floor

The sun must have got up very early. He was shining brightly through Yo's window and right on to Haffertee's face. So Haffertee was wide awake.

He climbed slowly out of the pillowcase and looked up at the shelf above the door. Howl Owl was still asleep.

He looked at Diamond Yo. She was a big bump under the bedclothes, and she was still asleep.

Haffertee took a look round. Nobody else was awake. There wasn't a sound from anybody. He went to the bedroom door and peeped outside. Not even the Purrswell kittens were awake yet. All three of them were curled up on the mat outside Fran's bedroom, fast asleep. Fran was Yo's big sister – and her bedroom door was wide open.

Haffertee could just see inside.

And what he saw made him shudder and look again. There was a leg on the floor. Not all of a leg but just the bottom part near the foot. It was very still.

Haffertee went over to look more closely. The closer he got the worse he felt.

And then when he got right up to the door he could just see a body. It was quite still, just hanging on to the edge of the bed. It was wearing a white nightdress.

Haffertee was scared. He felt sure something very strange was happening. He took just one more look to make sure he wasn't dreaming. Then he leapt back into Diamond Yo's room shouting at the top of his voice.

But the top of Haffertee's voice was not very loud, and Howl Owl only opened one eye, said 'Shhhhhh!' and went back to sleep. Yo just turned over and grunted.

Haffertee didn't know what to do. He scampered up on to Yo's desk to find something that would make enough noise to wake the family.

'The radio! That's it,' he thought. 'I'll turn the radio on.' He looked at the front of it. There were three switches. One of them said AM/FM. Haffertee tried that one first. Nothing happened. The next said VOL. and he turned that right round. Again,

nothing happened. The last one said ON/OFF, and
when he turned that one he was nearly blown off the
desk by the noise. The whole house seemed to be
shaking with the sound.

Everyone jumped out of bed.

The Purrswell kittens scampered off downstairs.

Howl Owl nearly fell off his shelf.

Yo's brothers, Chris and Mark, came running in

in their pajamas.

Ma Diamond appeared, wrapping her dressing-gown round herself as she came. Fran was close behind her.

It was Mark who reached the radio first and turned it off. 'Goodness,' he said. 'What a noise! Who turned that on?' Haffertee was still standing right in front of the radio, covering his ears with his paws.

'What *have* you been doing, Haffertee?' asked Yo, now thoroughly awake. 'Why ever did you turn the radio on like that?'

Haffertee quickly explained. He had to wake people up and get them to listen. There was a body in Fran's room!

'A body in my room?' said Fran. 'A body in my room! You must have made a mistake.'

'No I haven't,' said Haffertee firmly. 'Come and look!'

They all came to look.

There was no body in Fran's room.

'But I saw one,' said Haffertee, still quite certain, but nearly in tears now. 'The legs were on the floor and it was just hanging on to the bed. And it was wearing a long white nightdress.'

'I'm wearing a long white nightdress,' said Fran quickly, 'and . . . oh! Haffertee, you are funny. I've just been saying my prayers. I've a lot of work to do today and I've been asking God to help me. You must have seen me kneeling down.'

'Oh!' said Haffertee with a sigh of relief. 'Oh. I thought you were hurt or something.'

Fran came closer and stroked Haffertee's head.

'I'm sorry if I frightened you,' she said. 'I was busy talking and listening to God and I didn't know you were there.'

Haffertee felt a little bit ashamed of himself and hung his head. 'I'm sorry everyone,' he said in a small voice. 'I didn't think God was at home in the mornings anyway.'

'Oh, Haffertee,' Yo said. 'God is at home all day. Come on, now. It's a long time until breakfast, let's see if we can all get back to sleep again.'

And they did.

All except Haffertee. The sun was in his eyes. And anyway, he was much too busy thinking about God being at home all day.

Gerbil Jokers

Haffertee was standing outside the gerbil cage. Gerbils 1 and 2 were rushing about inside chewing and gnawing away at a cereal box. They loved chewing cardboard and used the pieces to make a nesting-pile in one corner of the cage. Haffertee loved to watch them.

Suddenly the two little animals stopped chewing and turned to look at Haffertee. Then, slowly, they came forward to the front of their cage and stood up on their strong back legs and snuffled their noses against the wire. For a minute or two they just stood there – looking at Haffertee.

Or were they? Haffertee began to think that perhaps they were not looking at him at all but at something – or someone – just behind him. Haffertee turned round. There was nothing behind him but the kitchen wall. And that was quite bare. There was nothing for them to see.

Suddenly the two little gerbils started waving their front paws and pointing. They were pointing at the wall behind Haffertee. There was no doubt about it.

Haffertee began to feel very strange inside.

Whatever were they looking at?

What was so very interesting about a bare wall that they had to keep pointing and waving?

At last he just couldn't stand it any more. 'What are you looking at?' he asked, politely.

The gerbils took no notice. They just kept waving their front paws and looking at the wall.

'What are you looking at?' asked Haffertee, in a much louder voice.

The two gerbils slid their front paws down the wire. 'Ssssshhhh!' said Gerbil 1 softly. 'Don't make a noise or it will go away.'

'Go away?' said Haffertee in surprise. 'What will go away?'

'That splay-backed Zampassa,' said Gerbil 2.

'Splay-backed Zampassa?' said Haffertee, not really believing his ears. 'Whatever is that?'

'There's one of them on the wall over there,' said Gerbil 1 excitedly, and in a whisper. 'Turn round very slowly and stand on your head and you will be able to see him.'

Haffertee very much wanted to see this new creature. So he turned round very, very slowly and

very, very quietly and stood on his head. He wasn't
used to being upside down, so it took him some time
to get his balance. Then he stared hard at the wall.
'I . . . can't . . . see . . . anything,' he managed
to pant. 'There's . . . nothing . . . there!'

'Waggle your feet a bit,' said Gerbil 2. 'And try
buzzing like a bee.'

Haffertee struggled hard to waggle his feet in the
air and began to make a noise like a bee. 'Waggle,

waggle. Buzz, buzz . . . ! This is a strange way to look for a splay-backed Zampassa,' he thought to himself. And his head began to hurt a bit.

Just then Diamond Yo came into the kitchen.

'Good gracious,' said Haffertee between buzzes. 'You're walking on the ceiling.'

Yo took one look at the smiling gerbils and one look at the upside-down Haffertee, and then she understood.

'Haffertee,' she said slowly. 'What are you doing waving your legs in the air and standing on your head? And why are you buzzing like a bee? Come on, now, stand right-way up and tell me what's going on.'

Haffertee was very glad to take the weight off his head and stop waggling his feet in the air. He felt rather dizzy at first, right-way up. He steadied himself till he got his balance.

'I was looking for a splay-backed Zampassa,' explained Haffertee quietly. 'You can only see them if you stand on your head and waggle your legs in the air and buzz like a bee . . . '

Yo just couldn't stop herself smiling. 'Haffertee,' she said at last, nodding her head and patting Haffertee's fur into place. 'Those gerbils have been teasing you, Haff. They love playing jokes on people and they really caught you, didn't they? There is no such thing as a splay-backed Zampassa, and even if there were, do you really think you could see it better by standing on your head or waggling your feet in the air, or even buzzing like a bee? Why weren't the gerbils standing on *their* heads?'

Haffertee didn't answer. He stood quite still and his head drooped lower and lower. He turned to look at the gerbils. But they had disappeared under a pile of chewed-up cardboard in the corner. He thought he could hear them twittering.

It was too much! He shot out of the kitchen and up the stairs. Yo could hear him sobbing quietly as he went. Haffertee was feeling very silly and very sorry for himself.

He was still sniffing a bit when Yo went up to bed. He didn't like being made to look silly, and he still felt cross with the gerbils.

Yo said her prayers, mentioning Haffertee rather loudly. Then she settled down in bed.

'Haffertee,' she said quietly, after a moment or two. 'You mustn't be too upset about what happened. Those gerbils are real jokers. They love to tease and play tricks. But they only do it for fun.'

Haffertee didn't think it very funny, and he said so.

'Come on,' said Yo gently, scratching Haffertee's tummy. 'Nothing's broken is it? Your head is still on, isn't it? Your legs may be a bit stiff in the morning, I suppose, but it's not really as bad as all that.'

Haffertee tried not to smile the smile that was twitching at the corners of his mouth. But he couldn't do it. The twitch became a smile and the smile became a grin, and he began to chuckle.

Then Haffertee and Yo laughed and laughed and laughed. They laughed till it hurt. And Haffertee was laughing at himself!

Thief!

There was something the matter with Diamond Yo. She kept on walking round and round the room. Every now and then she would bend right down to look under the desk, or under the bed. She even got down on her knees and patted the carpet!

And Howl Owl was doing some strange things too. He was flipping and flapping and hooting and tooting all over the place – up on the shelves and round by the window and on past the cupboards. The two of them were certainly acting strangely.

'You are making me quite dizzy,' said Haffertee at last. 'Tell me what you are doing. Perhaps I can help.'

Yo stopped walking round and round like a clockwork doll.

Howl Owl stopped flapping about like a crazy bird.

They both turned to look at Haffertee.

'We are looking for two chocolates which have gone from my box,' said Yo firmly. 'From the box Mrs Fenner brought me yesterday when I had to stay in because I had a cold.'

'Chocolates,' said Haffertee. 'Chocolates? I

haven't seen any chocolates.'

Yo showed him the box. 'Two of them are missing,' she said, staring straight at Haffertee. 'Are you sure you haven't seen them?'

Haffertee was beginning to feel a little bit frightened.

'Haffertee,' said Yo. 'Show me your whiskers.'

'My whiskers,' said Haffertee in surprise. 'Show you my whiskers? Whatever for?'

'Come on,' said Howl, joining in the frightening. 'Let's see your whiskers.'

Haffertee stepped closer so that Yo could look at them. Howl Owl fluttered nearer, peering closely at Haffertee's face. And the two of them inspected his whiskers.

At last Yo spoke, slowly and solemnly. 'Haffertee,' she said. 'There's chocolate on your whiskers.'

'Yes,' mumbled Howl. 'There *is* chocolate on your whiskers.'

Haffertee couldn't believe it. 'There can't be,' he stammered. 'I haven't touched your chocolates. Honestly, Yo.'

'Haffertee,' said Yo again, very solemnly. 'You stole my chocolates, didn't you? . . . Come on now, own up. You didn't tell the truth, did you? . . .'

Haffertee couldn't understand how the chocolate had got on his whiskers. He hadn't stolen the chocolates. He knew he hadn't. But he couldn't make Yo and Howl believe him. He felt quite sick. Yo had never spoken to him like this before.

He began to cry. 'I . . . didn't take . . . the . . . chocolates,' he sobbed. 'I didn't! I didn't!' And he ran from the bedroom.

Down the stairs he stumbled and through the kitchen and out into the back garden. He clambered up the steps to the very top of the garden and under the wire fence into the Bramble Wilderness. He was never ever going back to Hillside House again. As long as he lived . . . never . . . never . . . never . . . And he crouched down in a hole under a large mossy stone and the tears poured down his puffy cheeks.

Yo came slowly down the stairs. In the kitchen she found Ma Diamond making a chocolate cake. 'Hello!' said Ma as Yo came in. 'What's the matter?'

'Did you see Haffertee come through here a little while ago?' asked Yo.

'No,' said Ma Diamond. 'I've been busy with this cake. But he was down here half an hour ago. I gave him some of this cake mix. He *did* enjoy it.'

Yo stood quite still. 'You gave him some of that cake mix?' she said very slowly.

'Yes,' said her mother. 'He had two lots because he liked it so much, and I had to wipe his whiskers clean when he had finished.'

'Oh dear,' said Yo. 'Oh dear! I think I've made a dreadful mistake.' Then, without stopping to explain, 'I must go and find him at once.' And she rushed up to her bedroom to put on her shoes.

That was when she found the chocolates!

Her feet squelched right on to them, inside her shoes. What a chocolaty mess! They had fallen out of the box and into her shoes and no one had thought of looking there.

'Oh dear,' said Yo again. 'Oh dear! I *must* find him now, before it gets dark.'

It was very nearly dark when they found him at last. Everyone was looking. Ma and Pops, Chris and Fran and Mark, Howl Owl and Yo. All round the garden . . . And all through the Bramble Wilderness behind the wire fence. Yo found Haffertee there at last. He'd been getting colder and colder and lonelier and lonelier and he was still crying. Her very own Haffertee Hamster Diamond, in a hole under a mossy stone.

'Haffertee,' said Yo, very gently. 'Haffertee, I am so sorry. I called you a thief and I said you told lies and now I know I was quite wrong . . . I am so sorry.'

'And so am I,' hooted Howl Owl, appearing suddenly from behind a bush. 'So am I.'

Haffertee looked at them both through his tears. He was *so* glad they had found him. So very, very

glad. When Yo picked him up he snuggled down warmly against her neck.

'Friends again?' asked Yo, quietly.

'Yes,' said Haffertee. 'Friends again!' And together they set off for home.

Friends
All Round the Room

Haffertee woke next morning snug in his pillowcase as usual. He shivered as he thought of the hole
under the mossy stone out there in the Bramble
Wilderness.

How cold and lonely he had been – and how glad
to see Yo! And Yo had said she was sorry. That
made Haffertee feel very grown up.

Sleepily he thought about all that had happened
since the day he had tried to jump like a kitten. Being
a hamster was much better, he decided. It was much
more comfortable, too.

Then there was that Dreadful Fire. He didn't

like to think about that. Much nicer to remember Frank the Tank and Ginger Nutt.

What a lot had happened. And how much he had learnt! No wonder he was beginning to feel grown up.

Suddenly he remembered his Very Own Box. A place of his own. He hummed the song to himself.

> It's nice to have a cardboard box
> To call my very own.
> To leave my friends and all outside
> And sit here in my brand-new home.
> Who's afraid in a cardboard box
> The place I come to rest.
> My own bed and my own armchair.
> That's what I love best.

'Quite right,' he said firmly, as he finished humming. 'Quite right. It's time I had another look at my box.'

He wriggled out of the pillowcase and scampered

across the floor. There, by the door, was his Very Own Box. Haffertee took a long, considering look at it, and went inside. It *was* rather nice. But he still didn't like being on his own at nights!

'The gerbils sleep on their own at night,' he thought to himself. 'I'll talk to them about it.'

Gerbils 1 and 2 had run out of practical jokes for the moment, and were only too glad to chat.

'You see,' Haffertee explained, 'I like my Very Own Box in the daytime, but it's lonely at night when the lights go out. Can you help?'

Gerbil 2 stopped chewing for a moment. 'If you don't want to be lonely,' he said, 'make sure there are always two of you.'

'But how can I do that?' said Haffertee, a little crossly.

'Why not put up some pictures,' said a voice from the other side of the kitchen table. Pops Diamond had just come in from the garden and was washing his hands.

'Pictures?' said Haffertee. 'Pictures of what?'

'Pictures of friends,' said Pops, putting the towel back on the rack. 'There's that lovely coloured picture of you and Howl Owl for a start. I'm sure you could find pictures of all your friends if you tried. Here is a picture of Ma and me. You can stand that on your table if you like.'

Haffertee took the picture and looked at it. 'That's nice,' he said. 'Thank you very much.' And he went back upstairs deep in thought.

Yo was awake now, sitting up in bed reading her comic. And Howl was twittering away, trying to smoothe his feathers.

'Hello!' said Haffertee, as he came into the room. 'Can I have some pictures of the two of you?'

Yo put down her comic. Howl Owl's head emerged from his feathers and he blinked his two big eyes. 'Pictures?' they said together.

'Yes,' said Haffertee. 'I want to sleep in my Very Own Box and not feel lonely. Pops says you can't feel lonely with pictures of your friends.'

Yo thought about that for a moment.

Howl blinked about it for a moment.

'That's a very good idea,' Yo said. 'I'll see if I can help you find some pictures and we'll put them in your Very Own Box.'

'I'll help, too,' said Howl in his deep voice. 'I like looking at pictures.'

Before long they had found a picture of Howl on his shelf and one of Diamond Yo in the back garden. Yo drew a special picture of Frank the Tank. Then she hurried down to the kitchen. Mark and Fran and Chris all came in while she was gone with pictures of themselves. So, when Yo came back carrying a picture of the three Purrswell kittens *and* of the gerbils, Haffertee was delighted.

He spent a long long time arranging and re-arranging the pictures on his wall and his table. When he had finished, his Very Own Box was crowded with friends!

'Just one thing more,' called Yo, as he stood back to admire his work. 'Here is the mirror from my desk. You shouldn't feel lonely with all those friends, but if ever you do you can look in the mirror.' Yo laughed. 'You might even have a chat with Ginger Nutt!'

'Lovely,' breathed Haffertee, thinking of what Gerbil 2 had said. 'Then there'll be two of us.'

'Not two,' said Yo. 'Three!'

'Three,' said Haffertee in surprise. 'Who is the third?'

'God,' said Yo. 'Remember, he is always with you.'

'God,' said Haffertee, softly. 'But how will he get through the door?'

Yo smiled. It did look a rather small door.

'Oh! He'll find a way,' she said confidently. 'He

usually does!'

So, when it was time for bed, Haffertee didn't climb into Yo's pillowcase. Instead, he settled down on the soft warm duster in the corner of his Very Own Box. He looked round at all his friends and he wasn't afraid any more.

He had a good laugh with the gerbils.

Frank the Tank made him feel so warm.

He looked from Ma Diamond to his smart blue coat, and he could almost hear the whirr of the sewing-machine.

'Goodnight Howl. Goodnight Yo,' he whispered to the pictures on the wall. 'I'll see you again in the morning.'

His eyes were beginning to close when he remembered –

'Oh! and goodnight, God,' he said, quickly. 'I hope you don't feel lonely without any pictures!' And with that he fell fast asleep.

The
Diamond
Family

Fran   Ma

Diamond Yo
with
Hafferkee and
Howl Out

Pops

Mark

Chris.